What Can I Be Today?

Andy Gutman

First published by Dog Ear Publishing
4011 Vincennes Road
Indianapolis, IN 46268
www.dogearpublishing.net

ISBN: 978-145756-784-1

This book is printed on acid-free paper.
Printed in the United States of America

What can I be today?

What will I pretend when I go out to play?

What can I be today?

Come join me and we all can play!

I can be anything I want to be.

Started out as a caterpillar in a tree

Now a butterfly look at what it's taught me

I have so much potential inside of me
I can be a teacher and sing the a,b,c's

I can be a fireman; save a cat in a tree

I can be a sailor and sail the sea
I can do it all just you wait and see

What can I be today?

What will I pretend when I go out to play?

What can I be today?

Come join me and we all can play!

I can work on computers as a part of IT

Just you look out and wait and see

I can be a lawyer and protect the innocent

I can be a landlord and collect all the rent

I can work on a building and mix cement

I can be an explorer and live in a tent

I can be a doctor and work on a cure

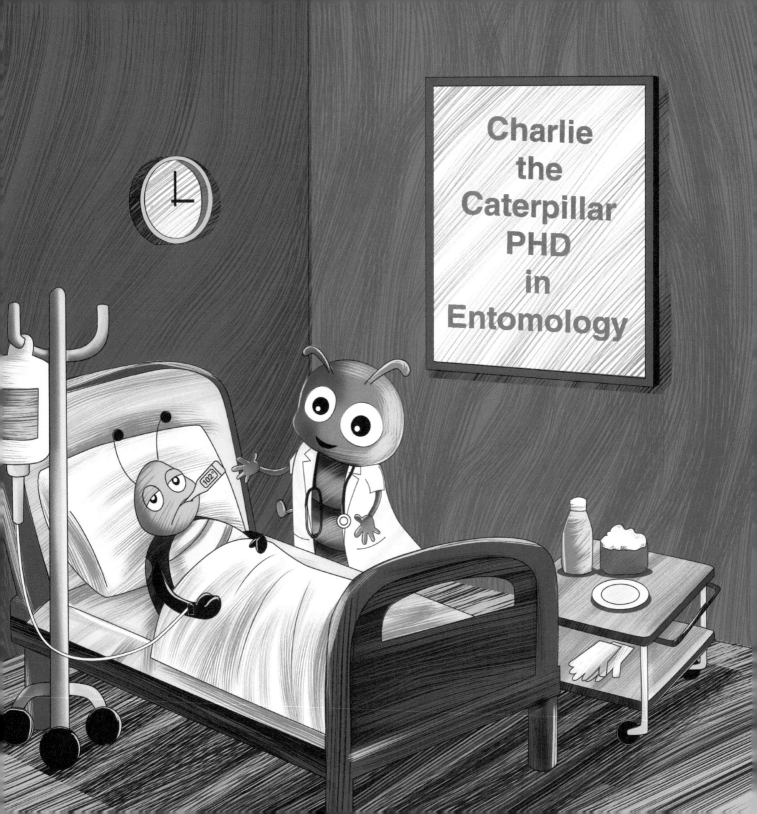

I can be a rock star and go out on tour

I can work with animals in the zoo

So tell me how about you?

Draw what you want to be

If I put my mind to it I know I can do it

Anything I want if I'm willing to go through it

What else can Charlie be?
Color in what you think he should be!

What else can Charlie be?
Color in what you think he should be!

CPSIA information can be obtained
at www.ICGtesting.com
Printed in the USA
BVHW021158210619
551571BV00001B/1/P